THIS BOOK BELONGS TO

**To Becksy – Because life is about
friends, old and new.**

First published in Great Britain 2021 by Farshore
An imprint of HarperCollins*Publishers*
1 London Bridge Street, London SE1 9GF

farshore.co.uk

HarperCollins*Publishers*
1st Floor, Watermarque Building, Ringsend Road
Dublin 4, Ireland

Text copyright © Farshore 2021
Interior illustration copyright © Dynamo 2021
The moral rights of the author and illustrator have been asserted.

Special thanks to Rachel Delahaye
With thanks to Speckled Pen for their help in the development of this series.

ISBN 978 0 7555 0130 4
Printed and bound in the UK using 100% renewable electricity at CPI Group (UK) Ltd

1

A CIP catalogue record for this title is available from the British Library.

MIX
Paper from
responsible sources
FSC™ C007454

CONTENTS

CHAPTER ONE

All Aboard the Ramen Ride!

It was morning in the World of Cute and honey-coloured sunshine streamed through the bedroom window of Dee the dumpling kitty. She yawned and reached for her wakey-cakey – a delicious strawberry and cream-filled donut topped with popping candy. She took a large

1

bite, and with a pop on her tongue and a tingle in her tum, she began to fill with energy.

Dee needed all the energy she could get. She had been up late, crafting, and her mind had refused to go to sleep as it was buzzing with the excitement of tomorrow.

Now tomorrow was today!

She stretched out her paws and then leaped out of bed. Pinned to the cork board above her crafting desk were the sashes and bows she'd made the night before. And stacked on the tabletop were little caps, each embroidered with the letters CC.

'Camp Cute!' Dee cried with happiness. 'It's time to go to Camp Cute!' She rolled around on the floor with excitement and then jumped to her feet. 'What am I thinking? There's no time to lose. I have to pack!'

Dee never went anywhere with empty pockets. You never knew when something might need making, or fixing, or decorating. And this weekend it was *extra* important. She and her friends, the super cutes, were on their way to Camp Cute Adventure School, where there would be activities and adventures and lessons about caring for the environment. They'd be staying the night, too. Emergency crafting supplies were essential.

Dee gathered balls of wool. She folded felt squares and rolled up materials and pushed

them deep into her pockets. She collected her brushes and pouches of paint. And what about clay? And glue and pins and sequins? Today of all days, she didn't want to run out of supplies. She pushed and packed everything as tightly as she could, but it was no good.

Although her fluffy pockets were deep and stretchy, they couldn't carry everything.

'Oh, I can't make it fit!' she wailed.

Make it . . . That was it!

'If you can't make something happen, then make something that'll help!' Dee exclaimed to herself.

She scoffed the rest of the wakey-cakey and licked the crumbs from her whiskers. Then she grabbed some quick-drying clay. Working quickly with her paws to pull, stretch and shape it, she created a lightweight box. Then she added canvas straps. Hmm. It wasn't quite good enough . . .

5

A second later, with the help of some paints, Dee had turned the box into a sturdy rainbow-coloured backpack!

'That's better!' Dee said. 'Ready, set, go!'

Dee placed her crafting materials inside the bag and swung it over her back. Then she clipped the bows she'd made all over her fur.

'Accessorising is everything,' she purred.

'CAMP CUTE, HERE I COME!'

Dee skipped all the way to the Wish Tree meeting place, where her super cute friends were already waiting. They clapped and whistled when they saw her coming.

'Hi, everyone!' Dee said. 'Sorry I'm late. I had to create!'

'You look amazing!' Lucky said, smiling.

'You do, too,' Dee replied. '*All* of you!'

Dee noticed that Lucky the lunacorn was wearing the rainbow-striped leg-warmers she'd made her for her birthday, and a tutu too! In fact, everyone was bright and colourful. Cami the cloud, Louis the labradoodle, Micky the mini-pig, Pip the pineapple: they all wore anoraks, bags and wellies in bright fruit-salad colours of pink, red, orange and green. Even Sammy the sloth had orange glasses on, and a compass hung around his neck.

'Here, I made you all something,'

Dee said, handing out the sashes and the monogrammed caps with their CCs.

'We look so C-C-CUTE!' Lucky laughed.

'Of C-C-COURSE we do!' Pip giggled.

'C-C-CAN we go now?' Micky said, pretend-seriously.

'Camp Cute, here we come!' Cami said, raining down little inflatable maracas, which rattled before bursting with a pop and a squeal.

'Let's go! Let's go!' Louis chased his tail in excitement, round and round. Pip had to turn him back the other way so he didn't get dizzy.

'Which way, Sammy?' Cami asked above the sloth's head.

Sammy opened up his map and traced his

finger along the route from the Wish Tree to a winding river that cut through the town and out to the wide sea where the hug whales swam.

'Here,' he said. 'Camp Cute Adventure School is on Sundae Island, right in the middle of Dragonfly Brook.'

'I've never been to Sundae Island,' Lucky said with excitement. 'It sounds magical.'

'It is,' Sammy said. 'You may be surprised to discover that I know a few things about the place.'

The super cutes groaned affectionately. It came as no surprise at all. Sammy knew facts about everything!

'Go on, tell us,' Cami said softly.

'Let's talk as we walk,' Sammy suggested. 'Follow me.'

They set off. Sammy sat on Lucky's back and called out Sundae Island facts, while Louis leaped and Pip cartwheeled. Cami tried to keep above the little pineapple to cast some shade. Pip was a hot-climate fruit who was scared of getting over-ripe.

'Did you know that if you get peckish on Sundae Island, you can eat the leaves of the yumyum tree – but *only* the green ones,' Sammy advised.

'Why only the green ones?' Dee asked.

'Because the orange leaves turn your wee orange,' Sammy explained. 'Which I suppose is fine if you want to have orange wee. There are also dandelion ducks as yellow as custard that nest around the shores. They're often hidden by the towering flowers, which grow much bigger there than they do in Charm Glade because of the special soil. It's fed by the sweet waters of Dragonfly Brook, which is enriched by hug-whale poo that washes in from the sea. Very nutritious!'

'Poo-tricious, more like!' Pip called, and they all laughed.

'And there are flocks of fluffy finches that come to roost on the island at sunset every evening,' Sammy went on. 'They sing themselves to sleep.'

'It really does sound AMAZING!' Lucky sighed.

The super cutes chatted happily all the way past the Smiley Sunflower Field and through Vanilla Valley until they arrived at the Museum of the Magic and Marvellous, which was full of fascinating facts and relics from the past. Micky worked there, and it was Sammy's favourite place. For the super cutes, it was also full of memories. Sammy had once hosted a sleepover party there which they'd never forget – full of friendship, fun and dazzling magic.

'Is this a trick, Sammy?' Pip asked. 'Have you actually just arranged another trip to the museum?'

'Maybe he's added hug-whale poo to the poo display,' Dee said, remembering the interesting exhibition that Sammy had shown her.

'No, no,' said Sammy. 'We're not going inside the museum. We're going round it. Trot on by, Lucky!'

The super cutes passed by the giant building and followed Lucky and Sammy across the museum gardens and through a hole in a hedge.

WHOA!

Behind the museum, hidden from view by tall hedge walls, was a little waterway with a jetty. A huge inflatable noodle bowl was waiting for them, decorated with streamers and balloons. It had the words *Ramen Ride* in swirly writing on the side.

'This secret waterway leads straight into Dragonfly Brook,' Sammy said. 'All aboard!'

The super cutes ran down the jetty and jumped into the *Ramen Ride*, which rocked from side to side. Even Cami and Lucky, who could fly, decided to take a seat on the inflatable. Cami liked keeping close to her friends, and Lucky was wearing her favourite wellies and didn't want them to fall off in mid-air. (Well, that was her excuse. She just didn't want to miss out on the ride.) It was all so exciting as Sammy took hold of the chopstick oars and rowed them

down the waterway and into the main river.

Dragonfly Brook teemed with silver butter-knife fish which darted between the lilac lilies where folly frogs sat, belching loudly. As the cutes neared, the frogs belched faster, and

their call sounded like a deep baritone chuckle.
Soon the super cutes were chuckling, too.
Louis doodled the scene on his sketchpad with
his clever pencil nose. Dee purred so loudly, it
sounded as if the *Ramen Ride* had a motor, and

that made the cutes laugh even more.

'I can see it!' Cami said in delight, pointing ahead. 'Sundae Island!'

In the near distance, the island's huge sunflowers and lush palm trees swayed in the breeze. And strung between two monkey puzzle trees was a large sign saying DOCK HERE.

'Just setting the course,' Sammy said, rowing harder. 'By my calculations, we'll be landing at the dock in about –'

ROOOOAAAAR.

Sammy's voice was drowned out by a wild growl. Coming up behind them was another vessel – although it wasn't a boat. It was a scooter. The wheels were fixed on to a large water-ski with a spinning propellor at the back. It ripped through the brook, startling the folly frogs and sending the butter-knife fish rushing for safety in silver waves towards the banks of the river. And riding on the scooter were four familiar figures – a pizza slice, an angry muffin, a snail . . . and a small chihuahua.

'It's the Glamour Gang,' Pip said. 'And Clive the chihuahua has got his nose in the air like he's king of the island!'

'Don't worry,' Lucky said gently. 'I can't believe he's already forgotten the lessons he learned at the Friendship Festival. He just likes a little drama, that's all.'

'You're not kidding,' Micky tutted. 'He looks as if he's wearing his entire dressing-up box!'

Clive was wearing a shiny gold waterproof and jewel-encrusted goggles that made his beady eyes boggle even more than usual. The scooter roared like a gargling lion as the Glamour Gang

tore by, churning up the waters and ruining the magical peace of the river.

'Careful of the dandelion ducks!' Cami shouted. 'They're nesting up ahead!'

But Clive lifted his head even higher and pretended he couldn't see or hear them.

The swell from the scooter pushed the *Ramen Ride* off course, back into the river, and the little boat drifted past the landing point at Sundae Island dock.

'Oh no! Where will we stop?' Pip asked anxiously.

'We'll find a way,' Lucky said.

'There's a beach! A beach!' Louis said, leaping from bench to bench.

Indeed, just round the corner from the dock was a shallow bay with a strip of sparkling sand.

'See?' said Lucky. 'Nothing is going to get in the way of us and Camp Cute.'

CHAPTER TWO

WELCOME TO CAMP CUTE!

The Ramen Ride floated into the bay and came to a stop on the shore. The super cutes tied their inflatable to a palm-tree trunk and hopped off with glee, into soft sand that squeaked underfoot. At once, they scattered to explore.

'A singing beach!' Pip laughed as she

cartwheeled across the tunefully squeaky sand.

The sun was beginning to beat down. Pip quickly took shelter from the sun under Cami the cloud. Louis ran in and out of the water, chasing butter-knife fish which teased him with squeals of 'Can't catch us!' Lucky went to see if she could find the dandelion ducks among the beach flowers.

'Look everyone, there's a sign.' Dee pointed to a post that had been hammered into the sand.

'Ah, oh dear, yes,' said a voice. 'Everyone STOP what you're doing!'

Everyone stopped. Then they looked around in confusion.

'Sammy?' Lucky called. 'Where are you?'

'What do you mean where am I? I'm right here!'

'I think you might be camouflaged, Sammy,' Cami called, gliding above them all. 'I can see a sloth-shaped shadow on the sand!'

'Oh, yes, sorry about that,' said Sammy, embarrassed. He often camouflaged himself without realising. He shook his fur, and the sand-yellow colour turned brown. 'As I was saying, we have to stop running around. If this is Turtle Bay, then the turtles lay their eggs right here in the sand. We need to tread very, very carefully.'

'Oh look – there they are!' Pip said.

She pointed to the other side of the beach, where a family of turtles was making its way down to the water for a swim. When the turtles saw the super cutes, they turned from green to purple and started covering themselves in sand.

'They're scared,' said Louis. 'I'll go and tell them not to be.'

'STOP!' the cutes shouted as Louis bounded towards the turtles.

'The eggs, remember?' said Lucky, beckoning Louis back.

'Maybe we should leave Turtle Bay in peace,' Sammy said, with a very concerned face.

'Yeah! Let's get going to Camp Cute!' Dee said. She was eager to get started on the day's events.

The super cutes made their way carefully up the beach and into the shady woods. Even Sammy wasn't sure which direction to go in, as he'd only drawn his map as far as the dock. Cami had to float above the treetops so she didn't get tangled in the branches. Luckily, from up that high she could see the whole of Sundae Island and was able to direct them through the woods.

'I can see Camp Cute, I can see it!' she exclaimed. The happy cloud dropped down little gummy stars which fell through the canopy and made a trail for the cutes to follow.

'I think Cami likes what she sees,' Dee laughed, trying to catch a star.

'Follow the star trail!' Cami called. 'We're nearly there!'

A delicious smell wafted through the woods, warm and sweet. The cutes looked at each other and licked their lips. A minute later the path petered out. Cami was waiting for them there, raining so many stars that the gummies made a glistening curtain. Laughing, the cutes ran through the gummies – and burst on to the main field.

There were yurts at one end, a firepit circle, and information stands for activities. Little paths criss-crossed through the grass. Metal arches covered in honeysuckle flowers created fragrant tunnels. There were flags everywhere, flicking in the breeze. The whole place was a riot of noise and colour.

CAMP CUTE

Cutes everywhere were getting started on their Camp Cute experience, being measured for hiking boots and collecting maps, compasses and binoculars.

'Look, there's the T-shirt stand!' Pip cried. With a leap of joy, she landed on her spiky top. Sammy helped her upright, and they went to fetch their T-shirts.

'One size fits all, one size fits all!' shouted Enzo the Easel. 'Come and collect your T-shirts! One size fits all! One size fits all!'

'How can one size fit all?' Louis marvelled, looking from Pip to Lucky, who were considerably different in height, width and length. Not to mention the fact that Pip had prickles and Lucky had wings.

'Magic!' Enzo said, throwing out shirts for them all to try on.

The cutes wriggled into their tops, and each one stretched as far and as big as was needed. A perfect fit, every time.

'I'm definitely taking a photo of you lot. You are SO cute!' Cardi the camera said, strolling over with a beam. 'Line up, line up!'

The cutes shuffled into a line, giggling with excitement.

'Now, after a count of three, say cuties!' Cardi said.

'One, two, three ... CUTIES!'

Cardi gave a big wink, which took the

photograph. The cutes cheered.

'The super cutes at the start of Camp Cute Adventure School,' Cardi said. 'We'll print out your photo and you can collect it at the end of your stay.'

'Does anyone get the feeling that this is going to be the best place ever?' Cami sighed happily.

'I thought nothing could beat the Blossom Festival at Charm Glade, but you're right, Cami,' Dee said.

'Or the Friendship Festival at Straw Breeze Field!' Pip said.

'But there's something so exciting about Camp Cute!' Lucky agreed.

'WATCH OUT!'

The cry came from cutes high in the air, descending on bubble-chutes.

They were being fired into the sky from a large bubble cannon at the far end of the camp field.

'I'm definitely doing that,' Louis yapped.

'We can play mid-air tag!' Cami suggested.

'What if my top pops the bubble?' Pip said nervously.

'If Pip's not doing it, then I'm not either. It wouldn't be fair,' Micky said.

'Let's check out what else there is to do,' Sammy said. 'After all, we're here to learn about the environment. If there's time left over for bubble-chuting, we can think about it then.'

'Before you get started, take one of these!' said someone. 'Oooh, my back!'

The cutes turned to see an elderly banana setting down a wheelbarrow filled with colourful notebooks.

'They're for you to write down your memories of the day. Because, believe me, you will be making memories,' she said with

35

a smile. Her eyes crinkled with loveliness. 'I'm Nana Banana, Camp Cute organiser, although I'm finding it hard to keep up with everyone. I'm not as green as I used to be. Getting more brown spots by the day!'

'Well, I think you look wonderful,' Lucky said, 'and if you don't mind me saying, you smell delicious!'

Nana Banana chuckled so hard her spectacles fell off and dangled freely on the chain around her neck. She really was like the most perfect grandma, and the cutes warmed to her instantly. Dee rummaged in her backpack and quickly knitted a little felt hat for Nana Banana to wear – lilac, which she thought looked good with yellow.

'Oh, that is delightful,' Nana Banana said, popping the hat on her head. 'And if you young ones need any help this weekend, just call my name. I may not be quick, but I'm the one to come to if you're not peeling well. I mean, feeling well.'

She winked and the super cutes laughed. A granny with a great sense of humour. This was getting better and better.

'Now, would you like to know where you'll be sleeping?' Nana Banana asked.

'Yes please!'

CHAPTER THREE

YURT MATES!

The cutes followed Nana Banana down a path that wove through fruit-floss stands and inflatable castles to a cluster of yurts on the other side of the field.

'Two in each yurt!' Nana said.

The super cutes chose the friends they were standing next to – Cami with Pip, Louis with

Micky, and Sammy with Lucky.

'What about me?' cried Dee.

'You're in that yurt over there,' said Nana Banana. She winked. 'And your camping partner has already moved in. Good luck.'

The other cutes rushed to make themselves at home. Dee tiptoed with uncertainty towards her yurt. All the yurts had different themes – Lucky and Sammy's was beachy, Louis and Micky's was foresty, and Cami and Pip's had a sweet-shop theme. But what – and who – was waiting for Dee?

She parted the drapes at the entrance and peered inside.

'Space!' she exclaimed.

She didn't just mean the roominess of the tent. The yurt material was deep blue on the inside and decorated with stars, moons and beautiful planets with rings and space dust painted in glitter. And on the floor were piles of suitcases and mountains of clothes so high, you'd need a space buggy to roll across them!

'It looks like I'm not alone in space,' Dee murmured to herself.

At the sound of her voice, a little head popped out from behind one of the suitcases.

'Clive!' Dee said, startled.

Clive the chihuahua bared his front row of teeth, which Dee supposed was a smile.

'Did you see us on Dragonfly Brook?' she

asked. 'You passed us at quite a speed. We tried to talk to you, but –'

'I don't know what you're talking about,' said Clive with a sniff. 'Where are the flowers? This tent is not fit for a diva unless it has flowers! This is so annoying! Pass me that pillow. And that one over there.'

'I think that's mine,' Dee said.

'You don't need two pillows!' Clive yapped. 'You've got a big head. My dainty neck needs lots of support.'

Dee decided not to let Clive wind her up. She gave him a big smile. 'Well Clive, you sure have brought a lot with you!'

Even though there were at least seventeen

outfits on the floor, the little chihuahua was pulling even more from another suitcase. Sequins, tutus, tiaras and LOTS of shoes. And then came the extras – snacks and cushions and nail varnish. Then Clive pulled out pictures in frames and popped them by his bed.

'My family is very important to me,' he explained, pointing at snooty-looking portraits. 'That one is my great-great-great-great-great-grandmother, Lady Sniffit of Waggly Castle. See? And of course Clawdius Cliveden, and my great-uncle, Barkly Houndsworth.'

'Wow!' Dee said, 'and who's –'

'And these are my cuddlies,' Clive said, quickly moving on to a bag of soft plush toys which he tipped on to his bed. He picked up an old lick-the-lips emoji cushion, worn and tattered, and propped it against his pillow.

Dee felt half tickled with amusement and half protective of this funny little chihuahua. It didn't take her long to unpack, and so she helped Clive arrange the rest of his toys and his accessories. Then it was time for the fun to start!

The other cutes were waiting at the centre point, chatting and leaping around. They had already been given leaflets which showed the island layout and its activities. There was Creature Care, Turtle Bay Tours, Bright Feather Reserve, Cloud Lamb Corralling . . .

'Do we have to do what they tell us?' Clive huffed. 'Everything is so organised, and I'm unique. I prefer to do as I please!'

'Sundae Island is a very special place and we're lucky to be invited, so I think it's best if we follow the itinerary,' Micky said sternly. 'Rules are there for a reason.'

'What shall we try first?' said Pip. 'I'm raring to go!'

'If I may suggest something?' Sammy said, stepping forward. 'As we very nearly had a turtle disaster on the beach, why don't we start with Creature Care? Who knows what other precious creatures might be on the island?'

'Well, you probably know,' Louis barked. 'You know pretty much everything!'

'It's true,' Sammy said, blushing. 'But it won't hurt to refresh my memory.'

'Creature Care it is!' said Pip, triple-tumbling with joy and landing with a thump, just missing a nervous stag beetle. 'Sorry, beetle!'

Standing beneath the Creature Care banner they met a flamingo called Franco, who told them all about the fluffy finches, and how to tell the females apart from the males.

'The females are brown with purple tummy feathers, and the males have pink tummy feathers and a blue crown. Such show-offs,' Franco tutted, stretching out his fabulous wings to wipe his brow before tucking them away again. 'Finches love sunflower seeds, and ideally they like to flock to flat surfaces. They're scared of the ground in case they get trodden on. So your first task is to make a bird table for them. See you later, feathery friends!'

Franco swivelled on one leg like a ballerina, puffed up his pink feathers and stuck his head in his armpit for a quick snooze before the next group arrived. Dee looked for Clive to see if he'd

had any thoughts about the activity. But he was nowhere to be seen.

'Anyone seen my yurt-mate?' Dee asked.

The super cutes looked around, but Clive had vanished. And then came a familiar noise. The whoops and shouts of the Glamour Gang.

'I guess Clive must have gone back with his old friends,' Dee said a little sadly.

There was a series of bangs, followed by the Glamour Gang's laughter as a flock of shy prickle-pears ran in terror across the field.

'They're letting off party poppers without thinking about the wildlife,' Lucky said crossly.

'I'm worried about Clive,' Dee said. 'I think he's a bit unsure about being away from home. Remember what he was like at the sleepover party?'

'He got over-excited and naughty,' Sammy remembered.

'Feeling homesick can make you a bit wobbly,' Pip added. 'I sometimes get homesick too.'

'Let's tell him that. It's nothing to be ashamed of. Whereas covering it up by being naughty definitely is!' Micky said, clapping his trotters together. Micky didn't like naughtiness on any level.

'Is everything OK?'

The super cutes spun round at the sound of lovely Nana Banana.

'We're fine, Nana,' said Lucky. 'We're just worried that Clive is getting carried away.'

'Well, then,' Nana said, smiling at them with her pretty wrinkly eyes. 'Perhaps your first task at Camp Cute is to find that little chihuahua.'

'Our first task is to make a bird feeder, though,' said Micky, who liked sticking to the rules.

'There'll be time for that later,' said Nana. 'You need to catch your friend Clive, before he scares away half the wildlife on Sundae Island!'

CHAPTER FOUR

The Soggy Lamb

A bank of rolling glitter-glue cloud was coming in from the east. A warm glistening mist floated on the breeze towards the super cutes and sparkles started settling on Lucky's horn.

'It's a glitter-glue storm!' Cami warned. 'And it's not coming from me.'

'Anoraks on!' Lucky cried. 'Glitter's really

hard to get out of your tail hairs.'

'And fur,' Sammy said. 'It'll ruin my camouflage.'

The cutes pulled their waterproofs from their backpacks and followed Nana Banana as she led them in the direction of the Glamour Gang's loud shouts.

'Footprints!' Sammy exclaimed. 'Clive was here very recently, look!'

There were dainty little pawprints in the glitter mist that had settled on the ground. Beside them were imprints from his Glamour Gang friends: the scooter, the pizza slice, the snail and the angry muffin. The cutes followed the trail, through meadows and woodlands, and past Sundae Island Farm – where they stopped, hardly able to believe what they saw in the farmer's field.

Sheepfrogs were leaping high in the air, rounding up scattered cloud lambs. The glitter sticking to the cloud lambs' wool made them look like magic candy floss.

'LEFT! HOP! RIGHT! HOP! HOPPITY-HOP! STAY!'

shouted the head sheepfrog. 'Wait for it . . . Come by. Come by . . .'

The other sheepfrogs leaped into positions that would herd the cloud lambs into a giant bubble. Some of the lambs were very spirited, and were refusing to do what the sheepfrogs wanted.

54

Lucky flew up to join the head sheepfrog. 'What happened?' she asked.

The head sheepfrog wiped his green forehead. 'A rowdy lot riding a scooter appeared out of nowhere and drove right through my herd, just as I'd finally got them all on the ground.'

Oh dear. The super cutes looked at each other sadly. Clive!

'I can help!' Pip shouted.

The little pineapple jumped as high in the air as she could. Unfortunately, her spiky top popped the bubble and the lambs that the sheepfrogs had managed to get inside all escaped.

'So sorry! Really sorry!' Pip cried, blushing. 'I guess me and bubbles don't go together.'

'Always better to ask for permission before leaping to help,' Sammy suggested gently.

The panda farmer had blown another giant bubble and the bouncy sheepfrogs were already rounding the cloud lambs up again. When they were all in, one of the frogs leaped high above the bubble and kicked it back down to the ground, where the panda was waiting to give the lambs

soothing cuddles. With their feet on the ground and their wool being stroked, the cloud lambs filled the air with gurgles of delight and happy sighs.

'He must be a cuddle puffle panda,' Sammy whispered. 'You can't get a better cuddle in the World of Cute.'

One lamb fell asleep and began to roll away like a woolly bowling ball. It gathered speed, heading towards the stream. The cuddle puffle panda farmer looked up, his arms full of cuddling lambs.

'Help! Can someone help me?' he pleaded. 'I'll never catch him in time. Every lamb is precious!'

The escaped lamb landed with a PLOP! in the stream and began to bob away on the current. The super cutes were horrified.

'I'll piggy-roll down the hill!' Micky suggested.

'No, the lamb will have gone even further downstream by the time you get there,' said Dee. She whipped out some coloured yarns from her pockets and began winding them together, creating a strong rainbow rope. She looped one end and lassoed it over Lucky's horn to use as reins. 'Come on, Lucky,' she said, leaping on to Lucky's back. 'Let's fly after that lamb!'

Lucky took off at once, with a very determined dumpling kitty clinging on to her mane. They flew downstream. Then Dee dangled over the middle of the river, her paws just touching the water, waiting for the lamb to arrive.

Soon the lamb came bobbing along, bleating with distress as it turned circles in the water.

'Come to me, lambikins!' Dee said. 'That's right . . .' Dee stretched out her paws and the lamb grabbed hold of them. 'Got you!' Dee cried triumphantly. 'Let's go, Lucky!'

Lucky flew up again, airlifting the cloud lamb to safety.

When they got back to the farmyard, the cuddle puffle panda puffed up his fur with relief, which made him look even more cuddly. All the cutes cheered. So did the cloud lambs – apart from the one that had rolled away. It was very grumpy. It was hard not to laugh as it stood, bleating flat notes of annoyance, looking like a pile of wet wool.

'Come here, silly lamb,' Cami said with a

laugh. She descended and wrapped her cloud fluff around the lamb and dried it as if she was a big fluffy towel. 'There. That's better, isn't it?'

'I'd like to thank you for rescuing my lamb,' the farmer panda said. 'Can I offer you one of my special cuddles?'

'Yes please!' said Dee.

'Me too!' said Pip.

'Me three!' said Micky.

But it was Sammy that went first. 'I need a cuddle and that's a fact,' he said.

After an enormous group hug, the panda sent them on their way.

'You've done very well,' he said as he handed out bamboo cookies to everyone. 'I will make

sure that Nana Banana hears about this and that

you all receive Camp Cute stars of achievement

for quick thinking and team work.'

'Speaking of team work...' Dee said, looking

at her friends. 'We'd better work out what to do

about a particularly troublesome cute.'

'Clive!' the other super cutes chorused.

'Yes,' said Dee. 'Clive is still on the loose!'

The super cutes waved goodbye to the cuddle puffle panda, the sheepfrogs and the cloud lambs – but they were suddenly interrupted by two post boxes running towards them.

Sammy peered through his glasses at the badges the post boxes were wearing. 'It's the wardens,' he said. 'I think something's wrong.'

The post box wardens – twins called Stompy and Stampy – screeched to halt in front of Nana.

'Chaos!' said Stompy.

'Crisis!' shouted Stampy.

'The island is in chaos and crisis!' said Stompy.

'The island is in crisis and chaos!' Stampy repeated.

'Calm down,' Lucky said. 'Perhaps you should use your breath to explain why.'

'Troublemakers. Noise, litter, haring and tearing about,' explained Stompy.

'They chased a terrified set of crayons into the tree. It took ages to get them down. And as soon as we did, they were scared right back up again. There are crayon marks all over the trunk,' said Stampy.

'And we don't know what's going to happen next!' said Stompy. 'Chaos!'

'Crisis!' Stampy agreed.

The super cutes looked at each other. This sounded like the work of the Glamour Gang . . .

'Where are the troublemakers now?' Cami asked.

The post box wardens shrugged. 'We have no idea.'

'Then I suggest we keep following the trail,' Sammy said. 'It'll lead us to Clive eventually. This way!'

'Don't worry! We'll find the gang and get

them under control!' Pip said with a flip and a sharp salute.

Stompy and Stampy nodded and scuttled away.

Sammy set off down the path. The other cutes followed in silence, faces creased with worry. Sundae Island was a special place of unique wildlife, with animals and plants that needed care. The last thing it needed was a naughty chihuahua causing havoc with every minute that passed!

CHAPTER FIVE

Feathers-A-Fluster

'Why do you think Clive is being so naughty?' Cami asked as they followed the Glamour Gang's trail.

'Remember, he's feeling a bit unsure. And he might be homesick,' Dee said.

'And he likes to be in charge,' Louis barked. 'He hates being told what to do and where to go.'

'It's a recipe for disaster,' Micky said. 'Remember when he threw a tantrum at the museum in a spiky cactus onesie?'

Sammy stopped and held his finger in the air. 'I can hear the call of a featherduster bird! Piffy-wit, piffy-wit!'

'What's the bird that's going wibble-boing?' Louis asked, cocking his head to the side.

'I'm not entirely sure,' Sammy replied. 'It could be the bouncing chaff. But with all this birdsong, one thing's clear – we must be near the Bright Feather Reserve.'

'Over there!' Cami said from her lookout above their heads. 'Straight ahead!'

A beautiful forest lay at the end of the path.

There was a sign beside a large tree which read:

'And the Glamour Gang's trail leads right into it,' Pip said with a frown.

The super cutes walked slowly into the forest. They gasped with delight at the flashes of colour in the treetops as birds dashed like rainbow darts between the branches.

'This is so exciting!' said Sammy, looking at the information board with its map of pathways and pictures of birds. 'I've heard about the birds in Bright Feather Reserve, but I've never seen them with my own eyes before. Now, here's a tip – hoods up!'

'Why?' asked Pip, just as a passing book bird dropped a large white splodge on to her head. 'Oh. That's why.'

The super cutes fell about laughing. Pip did look a sight. Cami gave her cloud fluff a squeeze, sprinkling a little rain on Pip and washing the book-bird poo away.

With hoods up and eyes wide, the super cutes followed Clive's pawprints through the reserve.

Every now and then they stopped to marvel at the incredible species that flocked and flapped around them. There were featherduster birds, just as Sammy had identified, with blue and pink feathers, rustling by with a cry of *piffy-wit, piffy-wit*, and white sherbet swans pecking across the forest floor.

'That's one kind of bird poo that

you do want on your head,' said Sammy. 'Sherbet swans do droppings made of pure sherbet. But we need to keep that a secret. Can you imagine if everyone found out? They'd be following the swans around trying to scare them so they . . . you know.'

'What's this?' Cami asked, floating towards a box on one of the trees. 'Oh, it's some sort of clock!'

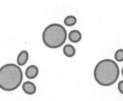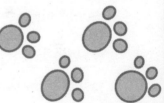

A cucu bird with a razor-sharp beak suddenly poked its head out of the hole in the box. And the clock began to chime.

Cami shrank back toward her friends. The rest of the cucu bird's body popped out of the clock. It flapped around in a panic before landing on Sammy's head. Sammy froze in alarm, which made the other cutes laugh.

'Don't laugh! Don't laugh!' the cucu bird cried. 'Danger in the Reserve. Noise and litter and flower pickers!'

'Flower pickers?' Cami quizzed. 'Why would Clive be picking flowers?'

'I know why,' Dee sighed. 'To decorate our yurt.'

'Save us, save us before the clock stops chiming!' the cucu bird shrieked as it flew away.

'What happens when the clock stops

chiming?' Lucky asked.

Sammy scratched his bottom. It sometimes helped him remember. 'When the clock stops chiming, it's siesta time,' he explained. 'All the birds

in the Bright Feather Reserve need their nap. It's how they get their energy for their sundown sky dance. But while they sense danger, they'll never be able to sleep. And they'll lose the ability to fly.'

'And what happens if they can't do their sundown sky dance, Sammy?' Cami asked worriedly.

73

'They can't meet up with their flying friends from all over the island. And they have to meet up with all their friends every evening, or their feathers lose colour.'

'Oh!' Lucky hiccupped with sadness. 'That's terrible!'

Dee flexed her claws with determination. 'That's it,' she said. 'We MUST find Clive, right this instant!'

'One problem, dear friend,' Sammy said. 'The pawprints and tracks have stopped.'

The friends stared at the empty path in front of them. Sure enough, the trail had vanished.

'So that means Clive must be somewhere near here,' Micky said. 'Let's split up and look for him.'

'But we'll get lost,' Pip cried.

Dee whipped several strands of coloured yarn from her pocket and tied the ends to the information post. 'Take a string each,' she suggested. 'Then you'll be able to find your way back.'

The cutes high-fived and set off in search of Clive. Sammy trundled into the dark forest and Lucky trotted towards the lake. Cami stayed by the information post and Micky and Pip wandered around the perimeter to see if there were any more pawprints.

Clive wasn't far at all. Dee found him sitting on the ground on the other side of the cucu's tree, with his back against the trunk. He was shaking, although she couldn't tell if it was because he was scared or cold or angry. The little chihuahua seemed to have an attack of the quivers for almost any reason.

'Clive, what are you doing?' Dee said softly.

'None of your business!' Clive snapped.

Although Clive's little bark was sharp, Dee thought she could hear something sad behind his confident woof.

'I'm your yurt-mate. That means you can tell me anything,' she said. 'Why don't you try? It might make you feel better.'

Clive looked doubtful. Dee settled down opposite him, quickly knitting away at a new snazzy jacket to lift his spirits. At last, he nodded his head very slightly.

'I've been a bit . . . well . . .' he began. 'I'm embarrassed to say.'

Dee nodded encouragingly. 'You've been running around, trying to take your mind off something, haven't you?'

Clive's bottom lip trembled. 'I'm a little upset,' he said. 'I thought if I was me times a hundred – a super-charged Clive – then the feelings would go away.'

'I understand,' Dee said. 'And where is the Glamour Gang?'

Clive sniffed. 'When I saw the clock, I sent them away. I wanted to be alone,' he said. 'I have a clock just like it. It's made me miss home even more . . . I didn't want them to see me this way.'

'But why didn't you just explain all this to the Glamour Gang?' asked Dee. 'You should be able to talk to your friends about anything.'

'They wouldn't understand,' Clive whined.

'Tell you what,' Dee said. 'Why don't you come back now and spend the rest of the day with me and the rest of the super cutes?'

Clive shook his head furiously. 'I don't want to see anyone.'

Dee had an idea. 'Try this on,' she said temptingly, holding up the jacket she had been knitting. 'It's one of a kind. No one else has one like this in the entire World of Cute.'

Clive took off his waterproof and slipped into the rainbow thread jacket, which Dee had studded with sparkling crystals. He batted his eyelashes. Then his eyebrows lifted and a smile crept across his muzzle. He did a little twirl.

'How do I look?' he said.

'Like a chic chihuahua who will brighten up everyone's day,' said Dee, laughing. 'Come and show the others.'

'OK!' Clive yipped, and Dee smiled to herself.

The other cutes had followed their strings back to the information point and were waiting, listening to the bongs of the cucu clock and worrying that the birds would never get to sleep. When they saw Dee and Clive skipping towards them, they breathed a big sigh of relief.

'Don't I look fabulous?' Clive cried. 'I'm the brightest creature in the Bright Feather

Reserve, aren't I? Aren't I?'

'You are,' Cami said sweetly.

'And now that we're all together,' said Louis, 'let's give the birds something to eat before they settle down for a siesta.'

'Fluffy finches like bird tables,' Lucky remembered. 'Let's build one now and complete Franco the flamingo's task!' She pointed at some logs and planks at the side of the path. 'Quickly, help me lift the logs upright!'

'Yes! Yes!' Micky said. 'Quick march, everyone. If everyone helps, it should be easy.'

They heaved the biggest log upright and twisted it into the ground. Then Pip took a plank, and, with a bounce and a flip, popped it on the top like a table. She tumbled back down, but thankfully landed in the pile of yarn that the cutes had used to find their way in the forest. Lucky flew Dee to the top of the bird table, where the dumpling kitty grabbed a hammer and nails from her crafting kit and fixed the plank firmly to its log post.

'Now we just need food,' Sammy said.

'I've got some dried berries,' Micky said, rummaging for the snacks in his pocket.

'I've got crumbs from some cookies I got from the bake stall,' Clive said.

With the help of Cami, they sprinkled the food high up on the bird table and stood back. Within seconds, the bright feathery beauties spied the goodies and began flocking, beating their wings, twitching their tails and tucking into a scrummy feast.

Apart from the contented sound of eating, the forest was quiet and peaceful, just as it should be!

BONG! BONG! BONG!

The final bongs from the cucu clock sounded, and the birds of Bright Feather Reserve disappeared again in a flurry of rainbows back to their nests and roosts, ready for their precious siesta.

CHAPTER SIX

Clive Sings a Different Song

The super cutes smiled at each other as they heard the piffles and wiffles of gentle snoring coming from the trees above them. The colourful birds of the Bright Feather Reserve were all fast asleep. But Sammy was looking troubled.

'What's the matter, Sammy?' Cami said,

floating down to the sloth's shoulder.

'I'm wondering how Clive and the Glamour Gang managed to get into the Bright Feather Reserve in the first place without being stopped by the ranger,' said Sammy. 'A protected area like this is sure to have a ranger.'

'Let's find out. Back to the information board!' Lucky cried.

The cutes rushed back to the board. Clive practised his pirouettes as everyone read the information again.

'There,' Pip said. 'It says the ranger is Matilda the merpuss.'

'Clive, did you see a merpuss when you first entered the reserve?' asked Cami.

Clive shook his little head and continued with his pirouettes.

'What's a merpuss?' Lucky asked.

'If I remember rightly, it has the head of cat, tail of fish . . .' Sammy began. He frowned. 'Or maybe the head of a fish and the tail of a cat. No, definitely the head of a cat . . .'

'But don't cats chase birds?' Micky asked.

'Not always,' Dee huffed. 'Some of us have more intelligent hobbies. Matilda the merpuss . . . I think that might be one of my distant relatives. I hope nothing has happened to her. What if she's stuck or in trouble?' Dee's eyes widened in fright. 'What if she's been kit-napped?'

Clive stopped his pirouettes, with his little

toes pointed towards Dee like a dancer. 'If there's one top cat-tracker in the World of Cute, it's me!' he said proudly.

'Sure it is, Clive,' said Pip, rolling her eyes.

Lucky nudged her. 'Be nice,' she whispered.

'Actually, it's true,' Sammy said. 'Clive comes from a great family of trackers.'

Clive smiled cutely at Sammy. 'Thank you.' Then he turned to the others. 'Finding Matilda the Merpuss is the least I can do, after ruining all the peace. I am sorry, you know. I just didn't realise how being homesick would make me act.'

There was silence. Had the haughty chihuahua just apologised? It looked like he had!

Lucky recovered first. 'We're so proud

of you, Clive,' she said. 'Admitting that you're wrong isn't always easy.'

All the cutes agreed and patted Clive, apart from Louis who whispered in his ear: 'It would be an honour to be your right-hand hound, Clive. Although my magic nose is better at creating than sniffing. But together we can track down this merpuss!'

Clive blinked happily. Together, the dogs put their noses to the ground and sniffed along a pathway that skirted round the Bright Feather Reserve.

'I wonder where the merpuss can be?' Cami said, as the friends followed Clive and Louis.

'We'll find her,' Dee said. 'It looks as if Clive and Louis have already caught a scent.'

Ahead of them, the two dogs had stopped. Their eyes were wide and their tails were sticking straight in the air. Then they started running.

'This trail leads to Rocket Beach,' Sammy panted, running after Clive and Louis with the others while peering at the map. 'What would Matilda be doing there?'

The cutes soon found themselves at the top of the Rocket Beach sand dunes. The dunes were covered with firework flowers, which gave the beach its name, and looked as if they were shooting into the air. But the cutes didn't have

time to stop and swoon, because Louis and Clive were on to something. They had dashed to the other side of the beach, where there were caves that tunnelled into the rocky headland. There they stopped and waited for the others.

'Inside there? Really?' Pip said, peering into the first gloomy cave.

'Ssshhh, listen,' said Clive.

There was a noise coming from inside. A soft mewing.

'Looks like you did find her!' Lucky said. 'You two are amazing!'

'Hope she's OK,' Cami said from above. She'd settled over Pip, who was ripening in the sun and struggling with the hot sand beneath her feet.

The cutes tiptoed into the cave, waiting for their eyes to adjust to the darkness. And then they saw Matilda. The merpuss was lying against the back wall of the cave with her tail curled round a little fluffy ball.

Lucky quickly shuffled the cutes back out again.

'What is it?' asked Micky. 'Has she stolen some candy floss and kept it for herself?'

Lucky laughed. 'No, no, no. I spotted something fluffy, but it wasn't candy floss. I think Matilda has just had a baby. A tiny new merkitten!'

'AAAAAAHHHHH!'

said all the cutes together.

'No wonder she couldn't take care of the Bright Feather Reserve. She had her paws full!' Pip declared.

Matilda appeared, smiling shyly, with her little merkittie cradled in her arms. 'I'm so sorry I left Bright Feather Reserve,' she said, trying to comfort her kitty, who was now squirming and mewing wildly. 'But there was a wild dog on the loose. I heard it running through the forest, disturbing all the wildlife. I was scared. I didn't think it was safe.'

Everyone turned to Clive. The chihuahua gave

a little cough and his cheeks turned red. He looked at the crying merkitten.

'I think the kittie needs a lullaby,' Clive said. 'You know, my forefather Clawdius Cliveden was a very good singer and I've inherited his talents.'

The super cutes weren't so sure. They'd heard Clive's singing, and it was terrible! But there was no stopping him. Clive leaned over the merkittie and began to sing.

Merpuss, welcome to our world

Did we make your tiny head whirl?

Not too much, now. Time to rest

Go back to sleep in your little tiny nest . . .

When he wasn't trying to show off and sing super loudly, Clive's voice was actually rather sweet. The friends looked at each other with pleasant surprise. The baby merpuss began to make little purring noises as her eyes closed. Clive had sung her back to sleep!

'Quick, build her a nest,' Clive whispered.

This was a job for Dee! She fluffed up her fur and set to work making a perfect bowl-shaped nest, sending her friends to find feathers for the lining. When it was finished, the nest was soft, warm and super snuggly.

Dee handed the nest to Matilda, who lowered the sleeping kitty into it.

It was such a beautiful sight that no one said anything for a very long time.

CHAPTER SEVEN

Trouble Bubbles

The cutes made their way back to the main activities field and grabbed pop-fresh juice from the refreshments stand. The bubbly fruit juice was just what they needed. It filled their tummies and made them sigh.

'I don't know about you, but this feels like friendship central!' Lucky said, beaming. 'What an incredible team. Just look what we can achieve when we work together.'

'Yee-ha!' said Pip, doing a flip and crashing into Sammy, who was scratching his –

'Poo for all of you,' Nana Banana interrupted, opening her hand to reveal some white bird droppings.

The cutes looked at each other, a little alarmed.

'It's from the sherbert swans,' Nana chuckled. 'I've heard some very good things about you. You are all true friends of Sundae Island. And true friends deserve a special treat. We don't give out sherbet swan poo to everyone.' And she winked.

The cutes popped the little white pearls into their pop-fresh drinks and the liquid fizzed and shot tiny bubbles straight up their noses.

'Dee-licious!' said the dumpling kitty, twitching her whiskers.

'Loving my POOP-fresh drink!' Pip said.

The cutes all laughed at each other's expressions, as their tongues tingled and their eyes watered at the rush of bubbling juice. All but Clive, who wasn't interested in his drink at all. He was staring at Lucky's horn expectantly.

'Why are you looking at me like that?' Lucky said.

'Because I know I did some bad things, but I've made them better now,' Clive replied, still staring at Lucky's horn.

'I know you have,' Lucky soothed. 'You did really well, admitting you were wrong. And you helped the little merkitty go back to sleep!'

Clive's face scrunched up with annoyance. 'Then why isn't your friendship horn bursting with confetti or glitter or sweets?' he yelled. 'If everything is perfect it would! You know it would!'

It was true. In the past, Lucky's horn had exploded with confetti and treats in a magical celebration when she felt the full warmth of friendship. But it was doing absolutely nothing now.

'Haven't I done enough?' Clive barked. 'Why is everything so hard?'

'Don't worry, Clive,' said Lucky. 'My horn doesn't judge people – it just chooses the right moment. You've put lots of things right, but this isn't about me. It's about YOU. Perhaps when you feel you've done enough to make up for your naughtiness, my horn will know it.'

'IT'S NOT FAIR!' Clive yelled. 'Your silly horn is broken! I hate you!'

Lucky gasped. The cutes stared in disbelief. What a horrible thing to say!

Clive's body began to tremble, from his tail to his nose and his ears to his toes. Just when it looked as if he might burst into a yappy ball of fury, Cami sat on his head and squished his ears flat, which took him by surprise.

'We all feel sorry for ourselves from time to time,' Cami told Clive firmly. 'But trying to make others unhappy is not the way to deal with it. Now apologise to Lucky.'

Clive's head was still covered in Cami's cloud fluff. His lip wobbled.

'Sorry,' he whispered, and then his mouth puckered as if he'd sucked a lemon.

Lucky nodded uncertainly. Clive's words had been very hurtful.

'Clive, is there anyone else on the island you might have been rude to?' Cami asked gently. 'Perhaps, when everyone has forgiven you, you'll feel much better about things.'

'It'll be embarrassing. No one will want to speak to me,' Clive grumbled.

'I've got an idea,' said Micky. 'Why don't you say you're sorry, using that brilliant lullaby voice? It really is very good. You could make up an apology verse.'

'Yeah!' Pip cartwheeled round Clive. 'No one could resist an apology song.'

Clive blinked rapidly. He turned to Lucky

and trapped her in his bulgy gaze. Then he sang.

I'm sorry that I did you wrong

And made you really sad

Please hear my apology song

I hope it makes you glad.

'That's lovely,' Lucky said with a huge smile.

'Good job, everyone. And very well done to you, Clive,' Nana Banana said. 'Shall we go and put things right?'

It was easy to tell who Clive had offended because when they saw him, they immediately tried to run away.

Wilma the whip started to run the moment

she spotted the chihuahua, screaming, 'Don't do it again! Please!'

Clive looked at the super cutes. 'I squeezed choc topping all over her,' he explained sheepishly. 'Wait! Wilma, please! I want to say sorry!'

The ice-cream slowly turned around.

Clive trotted up to her, struck a pose and began to sing his song. And as he sang, the cutes formed a circle and danced to lift the mood and make Wilma feel special. Wilma was so overcome with emotion that she started to melt, and Cami had to chill her down again with a blast of freezing air.

'She loved the song, didn't she?' Clive said proudly. 'It was pretty amazing.'

During the apology tour of Camp Cute, Clive approached the crayons he'd terrorised, Benito the buffalo whom he'd called a hairy whatsit, and Palma the pug monkey whose tail he'd tied to a hot-dog stand with disastrous results. There were also the traumatised post box wardens Stompy and Stampy, who were still shouting 'Chaos!' and 'Crisis!' Clive sang his song and the cutes danced and cheered, and soon everyone was having such a good time, they had quite forgotten the unpleasant parts of the day.

Clive's final apology was to a cuddly pea pod called Poppy, who had been weeping because she was homesick. Clive had called her a cry baby. He sang her his song and when he'd finished, he whispered in her ear, 'I'm scared of being away from home too.' Poppy smiled and blinked and then the pea pod and the chihuahua danced with the rest of the cutes round and round and round until they all got so dizzy they fell over.

Micky noticed the little dog's cheeks looked a little green. 'Are you all right, Clive?' he asked.

'Getting dizzy confuses the body's balance and that can make you feel sick,' Sammy said, looking at his own bright green fur.

'Actually,' gulped Clive, 'it's not the dancing that's made me feel ill.'

'What is it, then?' Pip said.

'It the CUTENESS!' Clive wailed. 'Everything is so cute it's making me feel ill!'

The super cutes all fell back down, rolling on the ground with laughter – apart from Cami, who hovered above them all and spread her cloud fluff to keep the sun out of their eyes.

Nana Banana straightened her glasses and her felt hat. 'And that's the truth,' she said. 'Now, everyone on your feet. Evening will be on us soon, and there's lots of friendship treats to go before bedtime. But before we get ready, perhaps Clive would like to tell us if he's learned any lessons today?'

Clive dusted himself down and did a little

cough. 'I have learned that . . . sad rhymes with glad.'

The group of cutes stared at him. He was not going to get away with that! Clive looked down and muttered into his rainbow sparkle jacket.

'CAN'T HEAR YOU!' the super cutes shouted.

'Go on,' Dee said, patting Clive with a soft paw. 'The truth doesn't hurt as much as you think it does.'

Clive sighed. Then he said clearly, 'I learned that you should be kind to your neighbours.'

'Wonderful. A big Camp Cute Adventure School star goes to you, Clive,' Nana said. 'Now, as an orienteering task, you have to find your way back to the yurts. Better do it quickly – we don't want to miss the birds' sundown sky dance.'

The cutes looked around them. Where were they? How would they get back?

Sammy fiddled with his compass and turned in circles. Clive sniffed loudly.

'Don't cry, it's all going to be OK,' said Dee.

'I'm not crying, I'm smelling,' Clive said.
'And I can smell roasting marshmallows *and*
it's coming from somewhere over there.' He
pointed west. 'Follow me, everyone!'

'He's right,' Louis said, sticking his nose in
the air. 'Well done, Clive!'

CHAPTER EIGHT

A Perfect Picture

Back at camp the cutes rushed to change into their pyjamas, whooping and singing.

When they got to the space yurt, Clive dashed in ahead of Dee. To her surprise and delight, it wasn't because he wanted to be first. He wanted to tidy up! He made room on the tent floor, folding his clothes and straightening up

Dee's bed. He even replaced the pillow he had taken. Then he stood back and looked at the dumpling kitty with a nervous smile on his lips.

'There you go, yurt-mate,' he said. 'It's funny isn't it, how you're a cat and I'm a dog.'

Dee giggled. 'It is a bit.'

'Doesn't matter what you are when you're friends, does it?' Clive said carefully.

'No, it doesn't.' Dee blinked away a happy tear. 'Come on, show me which pyjamas you're going to wear for the campfire.'

Clive jumped on to his bed. 'These ones. No, these ones. No, these ones!' He stopped. 'Which ones do you like?'

Dee laughed. 'I like all of them, Clive!

Maybe you and I should both wear our onesies?
It could be the costume for Team Space Yurt.'

'No! I think I'll wear my star PJs and best tutu.'

The super cutes met up at the camp fire
which roared in the middle of the stone circle.
There were log seats round the edge, a safe

distance from the flames which leaped and spat and hissed. They had blankets over their knees and achievement stars all over their pyjamas! They wrote some of the memories of the day in their Camp Cute notebooks, looking up at each other and smiling.

Clive left the campfire and tiptoed away, returning a few minutes later with the Glamour Gang and a smile as wide as the Marshmallow Canyon.

'Did you talk to them about how upset you were?' Dee whispered as they all sat down.

Clive nodded. 'They were really nice about it. Angry Muffin said he was sad, too. And Scooter said he wasn't just sad – he was wheely sad.' Clive paused and then grinned.

'Did you just make a joke?' Louis said, wagging his tail. Clive nodded and giggled.

'Write it down!' Lucky said. 'Write it all down!'

When they were done filling their books with

memories, the hot-water-bottle camp assistants
brought round mugs of hot chocolate,
plates of apples and toast with butter
and jam. And marshmallows, of
course, which they popped on the end

of long sticks. The super cutes dangled
them over the fire, then puff-puffed
them cool before eating them with
cries of 'YUMMY!'

When the chewing was done, Nana
Banana told them to put their plates and mugs
and marshmallow sticks on the ground.

'The sundown sky dance will be starting
any minute,' she said. 'So why don't we sing a
campfire song to pass the time?'

Camp Cute Adventure School

Where caring for nature's cool

We're so happy to work and play

Because that's what we do on a Camp Cute day!

They sang the verse over and over, grinning at each other because it was such a wonderful sound and such a brilliant night. Then, one by one they fell silent until it was just Clive's voice, as delicate as a bell, ringing out into the night.

We're so happy to work and play

Because that's what we do on a Camp Cute day!

It was so magical, Dee wondered if this

might be the happiest she could ever possibly be. But things were about to get even happier.

The birds were arriving for their friendship get-together.

Huge flocks of them were crossing the sky. Groups of fluffy finches, featherdusters, cucus, flute-toots, badgerwings and dippers. So many colours and calls, it was like a fairground in the air! Groups of birds stayed together, weaving in and out and round other groups like shoals of fish, creating patterns that sparkled across the deep blue sky. And as they sang and swooped, their feathers got brighter and brighter.

'WHOA!' cried the cutes.

Nana chuckled. 'Just you wait!'

As the sun set lower, more creatures stepped out from the darkness around them. Deer, weasels, horses and four-clawed bathtubs, which were a very rare sighting indeed.

'Everyone likes us!' Clive said, the reflection of the fire flickering in his eyes.

Dee looked at the chihuahua and smiled.
She hoped he was really enjoying the feeling.
He probably hadn't felt it very often. A feeling
like that could change a cute.

'There's Matilda!' Pip pointed out the
merpuss, carrying the nest they'd made with a

happy snoozing merkitten inside.

'And the cuddle puffle panda and the sheepfrogs!' Micky said. 'It feels so long ago we rescued that lamb. What a day!'

'Hey, where's the spray coming from?' Cami cried as droplets flew across the sky, each one carrying a rainbow. The droplets drifted down, sending waves of warmth and happiness as they landed on the cutes' skin.

'The hug whales,' Nana said. 'They can't come on land, but when they feel the time is right, they send us their hugs on the breeze.'

Clive stood up, his face bright with hope. 'Does that mean the time is right?' he yipped. 'Does that mean everything is OK? Lucky?

What do you think, Lucky?'

The moon had come out from behind a glitter-glue cloud. Lucky took off into the air towards it.

'What are you doing?' Sammy called. 'There's a glitter-glue cloud over there, you know! You mustn't get stuck!'

Lucky laughed down at everyone on the ground. 'I know! I won't go that high. I just feel like flying a bit, that's all.'

As the moonlight touched her horn, it lit up bright as a beacon. Lucky flew with the flocks of birds, dipping and diving, and her horn pulsed like a magical glow-stick. She flew over the campfire and over the heads of her friends.

'Lucky!' Clive called. 'Have I done enough? Is the spirit of friendship working?'

'What do you think, Clive?' Lucky cried.

Her horn flashed pink and purple and blue. Out shot a fountain of treats and edible confetti, all shaped as feathers. The feathers swung down on the breeze to the cutes below, who snatched them from the air and gobbled them up.

'I'M SO HAPPY!' Clive whooped, dancing around the fire.

Lucky landed and looked at the chihuahua like a proud parent. 'He's going to be OK, isn't he?'

'Clive is going to be just fine,' said Sammy.

Torchlight drifted across the field. Someone

was coming. It was Cardi the camera.

'I've developed the prints and I thought you might like to see yours,' she said, handing over a bunch of photographs.

The cutes looked and smiled. It was them at the beginning of the day, lined up with big grins of anticipation, wearing their Camp Cute Adventure School shirts.

Cardi smiled. 'What do you think? Cute, huh?'

'I think we need to do it again,' Dee said.

128

Cardi nodded.
'OK. Line up just
as you did before.'

'No, not just as we did before,' said Dee.
'Because there was something missing the first
time. A very special little chihuahua. Clive, will
you join our photo?'

Clive pointed to himself.
'ME?'

Dee laughed. 'Yes, you
Clive! And all of the Glamour
Gang! Budge up, budge up,
there's room for everyone
in a friendship photo!'

Clive squished in between his

yurt-mate Dee and his trusty friend Lucky with the Glamour Gang lined up on either side. Cardi the camera made them stand still.

'On the count of three,' she said. 'One, two, three . . .

FRIENDSHIP!'

CAUSING CHAOS IN A WORLD OF CUTE!

SUPER CUTE

FUN IN THE SUN

PIP BIRD

Here's an exclusive extract of the next exciting Super Cute book, out NOW!

CHAPTER ONE

Mud Magic

It was dawn and the sun was peeping over the horizon, covering the World of Cute with a sweet honey glaze. It woke the chime birds, which tinkled like miniature bells across the sky. The crepe flowers slowly unfurled, crinkling and giggling as the rays warmed their papery petals. It was a perfect summer's day.

Micky the mini-pig opened the door of the Piggy-Wiggle Sty and sniffed the air.

He smelled the sweet fragrant puffs from the candy-cotton fields, and the fresh mown grass left by the night-time grass-snippers. But there was something else in the air, too. Something that made Micky grin from ear to ear.

The scent of baking.

Doughy deliciousness wafted on the breeze,

along with the growing sound of chitter-chatter and excitement from all corners of town. It was a very special day in the World of Cute.

Micky was just uncurling his tail, which had knotted itself in his sleep, when a herd of fruit squashies flurried past the Piggy-Wiggle Sty. The miniature strawberries, apples and kiwis were very bouncy.

'Hi, squashies!' Micky called, waving. 'You're very lively this morning.!'

'It's the Friendship Festival,' squeaked a kiwi. 'And we're feeling fruity!'

Micky laughed. 'You certainly are. I suppose I'd better get ready!'

The little pig inhaled the delightful air once again before shaking himself to attention. There was lots to do – lots to do – and if he didn't get a piggy-wiggle on, he'd never be ready in time.

The Friendship Festival was a party to celebrate the longest day of the year – the most summery day of summer. In a few short hours, the Straw Breeze Field would be a carnival of music, crafting, picnicking and playing.

The most exciting part of all was the Friendship Treat event. Everyone going to the festival took a treat for the Treat Tent, and a Special Guest – chosen on the day – got to taste every single treat before the crowds could help themselves. The treats could be anything, from fruit salads to ice-cream sundaes to banana splits. **WHERE FRIENDSHIP SHOWS, ANYTHING GOES!** was the festival motto, and everyone was encouraged to make their treats in the company of friends.

Micky, whose day job was guarding the museum, was very keen on rules. Although he was eager to get started on making his special treat, he had to wait for his friends, the super cutes. He looked at his pocket watch. They would be arriving any minute!

He suddenly felt a pitter-patter on his head.

'Oh no! Not rain!' he exclaimed, reaching up to feel the droplets. But his head was completely dry. What was going on?

Micky heard a soft giggle. He looked up to see Cami the cloud, blushing with joy, above his head. She was raining hundreds-and-thousands, and a few were stuck to her cloud fluff. She looked like floating candy floss.

'Did I trick you?' Cami said, still giggling.

'You certainly did, Cami,' Micky said with a grin. 'I thought it was going to rain on Friendship Festival day. That would have been a disaster!'

'Did you know it hasn't rained on the day of the Friendship Festival for over seventy years?' said a voice. 'Even then, it only rained for 9.3 seconds just before lunchtime and –'

'Sammy!' Micky exclaimed. 'That has to be you. No one else has so many facts on the tip of their tongue. But where are you?'

'Oops! Wait a minute.' There was a flapping sound as Sammy the sloth shook the green camouflage from his fur.

Micky laughed and then turned around as a wobbly cheer rang through the air. A pineapple came racing down the road, faster and faster, squealing with delight, with a scarf streaming out behind her.

'It's Pip! On rollerskates!' Cami said from her lookout position above. 'Stand back, everyone!'

Micky stepped aside as Pip rolled past at full speed, windmilling her arms. She was going so fast, it looked as if she might race right through Micky's garden and out the other side. But there was a thud, then an OW! and – rather suddenly – Pip the pineapple stopped.

She kicked off her rollerskates and got up. 'Oh, Sammy! I'm so sorry!'

Pip had crashed into Sammy and prickled him with her spiky top. He started scratching

his bottom. He had an itch there anyway, so it was quite handy.

'Hey Sammy, I'll scratch it for you!' said someone. 'I'm good at scratching.'

They all looked up to see Lucky the lunacorn on the other side of the hedge, with Dee the dumpling kitty sitting on her back. Dee grinned and flexed her paws to show her sharp claws. 'See?' she said.

Sammy chuckled. 'Thanks for your offer, Dee, but I've got my itchy bottom in hand.'

'It looks like it!' Lucky laughed, jumping over the hedge and landing alongside her friends. 'Are we all here, ready to make and bake our treats for the Friendship Festival?'

The super cute friends all held up their baking bags, bulging with ingredients for their Friendship Treats. '**READY!**' they cheered.

'Almost ready,' Micky corrected. 'We're just waiting for Louis, and . . .' He gave a sharp whistle. A row of piglets marched out of the house. 'Everyone?' said Micky. 'I'd like to introduce my brothers and sisters – Molly, Miles, Marnie, Mei, Millie and Madhu.'

'Hello Molly, Miles, Marnie, Mei, Millie and Madhu!' chorused the super cutes.

Everyone put on their aprons. Micky's siblings did, too.

'What shall we bake? What shall we bake?'

said the tiny pigs, squeaking and squealing and cheering.

Lucky tossed her mane. 'I'm doing cupcakes, and I'm hoping that my horn will cover them with glitter. I've got a feeling it will.'

'Of course it will,' Sammy said. 'It's friendship that makes your horn do amazing stuff, and today is all about friendship!'

'I'm going to do some lightning biscuits. Kapow!' Cami shot out a biscuit in the shape of a lightning bolt. It was snatched out of mid-air by a furry muzzle.

'Louis!' the super cutes cheered.

Louis the Labradoodle munched the biscuit and gulped it down. 'My icing pen is at the ready to help with decorations!' he said. The artistic dog twitched his magical nose, which could change into pens, pencils, paintbrushes and crayons of any kind and colour.

Enjoyed Super Cute? Check out these other brilliant books by Pip Bird!

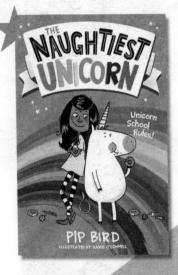

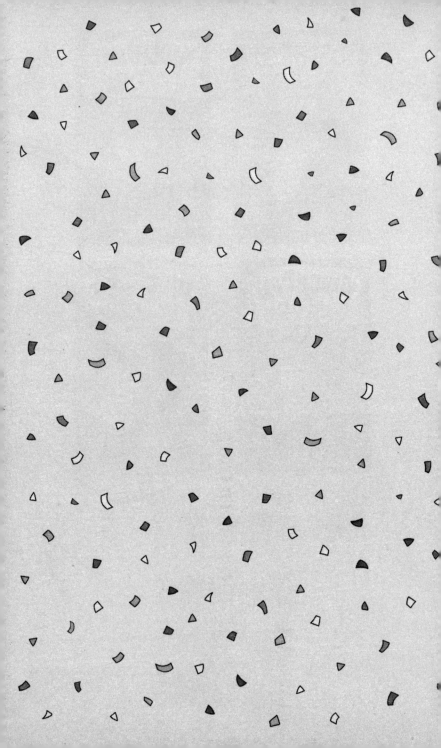